D0566762

Witch Twins
and
Melody Malady

DISCARDED

DISCARDED

ADELE GRIFFIN
Witch Twins
and
Melody Malady

ILLUSTRATIONS BY

Jacqueline Rogers

HYPERION BOOKS FOR CHILDREN

NEW YORK

LAKE AGASSIZ REGIONAL LIBRARY
118 S. 5th St. Box 900
MOORHEAD, MINNESOTA 56561-0900

Text copyright © 2003 by Adele Griffin
Illustrations copyright © 2003 by Jacqueline Rogers
All rights reserved. No part of this book may be reproduced or
transmitted in any form or by any means, electronic or mechanical, including
photocopying, recording, or by any information storage and retrieval system, without
written permission from the publisher.
For information address Hyperion Books for Children, 114 Fifth Avenue, New York,
New York 10011-5690.

First Edition
1 3 5 7 9 10 8 6 4 2
Printed in the United States of America

Library of Congress Cataloging-in-Publication Data on file.
ISBN 0-7868-1940-5

Visit www.hyperionchildrensbooks.com

For Emma and Charlotte

Contents

1
Double Delight

"GRANDY'S BRING-YOUR-OWN-Creative-Dish Labor Day Picnic Blowout is so crowded this year," said Luna Bundkin to her identical twin sister, Claire.

"That's because our family is growing," Claire responded. She and Luna were each balancing a paper cup of spicy peppermint iced tea in one hand and a paper plate heavy with fried catfish, curried rice, mango salad, and a strawberry-frosted cupcake in the other as they looked for somewhere to sit.

A free spot was hard to find. There must have been more than one hundred people milling around their grandparents' lawn or walking through the garden or relaxing on the sagging wraparound porch. Everybody was eating and talking and enjoying the fresh Bramblewine country air.

"There." Claire pointed to a sunny stretch of grass near Grandy's tomato patch.

"No. There." Luna pointed to a cool patch of shade under a crooked elm. "I hate to squint and chew." And she began to pick and weave her way around cousins, neighbors, and Grandy's cackling pals, heading toward the elm tree.

Luna could be stubborn like that, but Claire did not mind. She bounded behind her sister. She didn't care where she ate.

"More family is nice, but that also means more weird recipes," Luna observed as they settled on the grass. "Did you see what Steve brought? Lobster mousse with truffles on top.

It's extremely *eww!*" Steve was their mother's boyfriend. He was a chef at Aubergine, a Philadelphia restaurant so fancy that the waiters were often better dressed than the diners.

"On the other hand, Fluffy's triple-decker soy-butter, marshmallow, and pickle sandwiches on pistachio bread are yummy," said Claire. "Fluffy said it's a simple way of combining her favorite foods. She's sure got a big appetite, now that she's eating for two."

Claire exchanged a smile with her twin. In four months' time, their dad and their new stepmother, Fluffy, were going to have a baby. That meant a new little half sister or half brother for Claire, Luna, and their older brother, Justin. And Claire had a secret hunch that the baby would be a girl. A girl named Ubiquitous, one of the prettiest words ever, Claire thought. Ubiquitous meant "to be everywhere at the same time"—a next-to-impossible five-star spell.

You could just hear the magic in the word.

"Oh, lovely baby Ubiquitous," Claire said out loud.

Luna frowned. "Clairsie, everyone agreed a long time ago. Ubiquitous is not a good baby name. It sounds like what you'd name a Roman gladiator."

"Does not."

"Does so."

"Does not, no returns."

"Yoo-hoo! Howdy, there!" Fluffy was standing over them. Her plate was filled with triple-decker soy-butter, marshmallow, and pickle sandwiches. "May I sit with y'all?"

"Sure, Fluffy," they chorused.

"Thanks, gals!"

Fluffy, who was from Houston, Texas, often used words such as *gals* and *howdy*. Claire and Luna agreed that while they liked their new stepmother, it had taken time to get used to her. Fluffy was so different from their real mother, Jill Bundkin, who was a no-nonsense medical doctor. Fluffy talked loud and dressed in superbright, sparkly clothes, but everyone knew that underneath she had "a heart of gold."

Today, Claire noticed that Fluffy really did have a heart of gold, in the shape of a large, gold, heart-shaped belt buckle.

"I actually came over to ask you gals an important question," said Fluffy as she eased herself to sit on the grass between the twins. "Have either of you heard of Melody Malady?"

"Melody Malady!" Claire jumped to her feet, spilling her plate of food. In the next moment, Grandy's raggedy-eared cat, Wilbur, appeared out of nowhere and gulped it down.

Oblivious, Claire began to dance and sing. "'A tune of my own, and a person to be! Who is this girl? She could be only me! Believe it! Achieve it! Find your own Mel-oh-dee!'" She threw her arms in the air. "'For-ev-er me!'" Then she did a back flip.

Claire and Luna both loved-loved-loved *The Melody Malady Show*. It came on Friday nights at eight o'clock. In Claire's opinion, *The Melody Malady Show* was almost as good as her first-favorite television show, *Galaxy Murk*. Justin said no way. He said spaceships always beat singing.

"Yee-haw!" Fluffy applauded when Claire finished her back flip. Wilbur made a sour face. He was a witch cat and understood humanspeak, and he disliked *The Melody Malady Show*. Wilbur preferred Broadway musicals. (Being a country cat, he hardly ever got into New York City to see them.)

"You need voice lessons, Claire," said Luna, sticking her fingers in her ears. "Your singing is worse than mine."

Claire ignored her. "Why'd you ask about Melody Malady, Fluff?"

"Because Melody is filming a movie called *Double Delight* in Philadelphia," Fluffy explained, "and my magazine is writing an article on it." Fluffy worked for the style section of a magazine called *Philadelphia Now!* Both Claire and Luna thought it was a glamorous job.

"A whole movie! Does Melody play a

6

princess? Or a shoot 'em up cowgirl? Or a spy?" Claire was overjoyed that her favorite television star was on her way to movie stardom. "I *knew* Melody was destined for the big screen."

"As a matter of fact, Melody plays the double role of identical twin sisters, Jess and Bess," said Fluffy. "And I thought it might be some fun publicity if she got to shake hands with some real-live Philadelphia twins. So I volunteered to bring you two girls to the set. We'll snap pictures for the magazine, and maybe you gals can watch some of the movie being made."

"We're going to meet Melody Malady? Wow!" Claire could not think of anything more exciting than looking into the olive-green, almond-shaped eyes of her favorite television personality.

Melody Malady had been a star forever. Before *The Melody Malady Show*, Melody was the girl in all the television commercials for everything Claire wanted. Melody was the

Go-go Yogurt girl, the Sudsy Perfect Shampoo girl, and the Electric Wow Light-Up Jump Rope girl, just to name a few.

"Crumbs." Luna touched her hands to her hair. "I wish you hadn't cut my hair last week, Claire." It was a style the twins had seen in a magazine, and Claire had been sure she could copy it with her art scissors. The result was a clump of bristly short hair in the front and two clumps of scraggly long hair at the ears. "Melody will think I'm a dork."

"Aw, Luna, honey, it'll grow back," Fluffy reassured her.

Claire frowned. She thought she had done some creative and beautiful work on Luna's hair, but all anyone said about it was that it would grow back.

"When do we get to meet Melody?" Claire asked.

"How about this Friday?" asked Fluffy.

"Terrific!" Claire shouted. "Then, when we start school in two weeks, we'll be famous. Pictures of us in *Philadelphia Now!* next to the one, the great, the only Melody Malady! That's the awesomest way to begin sixth grade." She turned another flip from excitement.

Fluffy popped the end of her sandwich into her mouth, then stood and brushed the grass from her pants. "I'll go find your brother and invite him along, too. He'll probably be keen to see how movies get made. Glad you're excited about it! Bye, now, gals."

The twins watched as Fluffy went off in search of Justin.

"I wonder if Melody has her own hair-dresser?" Luna mused.

"She probably has her own beauty salon and her own maid and a butler and a Rolls-Royce and yacht and plane and a dressing room and an ice-cream parlor and everything," said Claire. "She's a star! And we're going to meet her!"

Luna slowly licked the pink frosting of her cupcake. "I read somewhere that in real life, movie stars are short with big heads, like Martians."

"No way. I bet Melody's got a perfect real-life head."

"Maybe she's spoiled and stuck-up."

"Luna, you are a doomsday prophet," said Claire. (That's what their mother always said about Luna.)

Her sister shrugged.

Claire would not let her twin get her down. She stretched out on her back and looked up into the elm tree's leafy canopy. This had been her most fantastic summer, ever. First she and Luna had spent five incredible weeks at Camp Bliss. Then came the news about baby Ubiquitous. And now she would get to meet her idol, Melody Malady.

Life did not get much better than this.

2
Animal Magic

LUNA HAD A SECRET. The secret was that she was jealous of Melody Malady. The reason Luna was jealous was because she thought it was too-too-too extra-lucky for a girl her very own age to star in a weekly television show *and* have a perfect singing voice *and* olive-green, almond-shaped eyes.

Luna was not even sure if she wanted to meet Melody, but she would never confess this to her sister. All through dinner, Claire had been chattering on and on like a squirrel about her idol.

Claire did not seem the *teeniest* bit jealous, so Luna did not want to seem like a spoilsport.

"I raise you three Oaty-oats," Luna said, yawning.

It was almost midnight. Luna and Claire were sitting at their grandparents' kitchen table playing five-card poker. They were betting Oaty-oat cereal pieces instead of money. The picnic guests had gone home, but Luna and Claire always stayed at Bramblewine for the first weekend of each month. It was a happy tradition, not only because they loved-loved-loved to be in the country with their grandparents, but also because it was then that Grandy, who was also (very secretly) known as Head Witch Arianna of Bramblewine, taught the girls new spells.

Claire lifted one eyebrow. "I'll see your three Oaty-oats and call you."

Luna showed her cards. "I have a pair of sevens. What do you have?" She was pretty sure that Claire had nothing, because she had been biting on her thumb. Claire always bit her thumb when she bluffed. Claire was not very good at poker.

Claire put down her cards. She had nothing. "Um, I was bluffing. You win again."

"After singing lessons, Clairsie, you should take poker lessons," said Luna as she swept up the pot of oats.

The clock struck midnight. The twins' faces turned solemn, and they stood up from the table and pushed in their chairs. It was time for their spell lesson. Tonight, Grandy had made the rare promise that she would be teaching them something "outstanding."

As they climbed the spiral staircase to the study, Luna could hear Grampy snoring from his bedroom. His snores rose and fell in perfect zzz-zzz-zzzs. Grandy had probably put him under a sleep spell. Luna figured that her grandmother must have cast it so that Grampy would not wake up during their midnight lesson.

Silently, the girls entered Grandy's candlelit study. All the green velvet curtains were drawn. The door locked and bolted automatically behind them. Witchcraft is a mysterious practice, and No Telling is its first rule. Although Grandy was a five-star witch and Luna and Claire were one-star witches, nobody else in their family knew. It was extra-extra-extra secret.

Grandy was seated behind her desk, scribbling on a notepad. Wilbur was flung out across the back of her chair. He was wearing his special rhinestone collar and trying to look noble.

"Shhh. One minute while I finish this grocery list," said Grandy. She jotted on her paper. "Dust balls, furniture unpolish, glass smudger. I just noticed how tidy this room is! *Blech!* A genuine study needs to look neglected."

The twins stood in the middle of the

room, waiting patiently. Their grandmother was not a woman to be hurried.

Finally, Grandy stood from her desk and swept to the middle of the room. Her dark witch-robe dragged behind her, and her shadow was so long it bent up into the ceiling.

"Hear this, witches mine. Tonight what you learn, you cannot return," Grandy intoned. Her face fell into its spell-casting expression, as she moved to stand between the twins. She raised her hands, palms-down.

Luna trembled slightly. On spell nights, Grandy seemed taller, bolder, and less grandmotherly than she did during daylight hours. Luna tried to look brave as Grandy began to chant:

> "We stand before this sacred shrine,
> To learn a new spell quite divine.
> Wipe your minds of thought and dream,
> Gather, garner, reap, and glean.
> Student witches, Wicca teacher,
> Transform to thine hidden creature!"

Then Grandy coughed three times into her hand. A pair of velvet curtains parted to reveal an altar, upon which sat two glass chalices, Grandy's Big Book of Shadows, a few odd jars of spices, and her crystal ashtray. The ashtray was not part of the magic. After a midnight spell, Grandy often liked to smoke a cigar.

On Grandy's signal, the twins followed as she glided to the altar.

"Eyes closed, mind open," Grandy commanded.

Luna closed her eyes. At her side, she wondered if Claire was peeking. She heard her grandmother cutting free some of the spices from their pots. She sniffed. Luna's sense of smell was terrible. She could detect only a whiff of spice mingling with something sweet.

Soon, the scent of spices was strong and made Luna's head whirl. In another moment, some rather odd changes began to brew inside her. First her skin got warm. Then her sense of hearing became needle sharp, even picking up the hum of Wilbur's purr and the zzz-zzz-zzz of Grampy's snores below. Finally, her legs seemed too weak to hold up her weight.

Luna dropped comfortably to all fours, her hands planting squarely on the carpet. All of this was confusing, but not nearly as odd as Luna's sudden urge to run and run and run and run! But she hated running! In fact, she hated any activity that got her sweaty. No, she was not feeling like herself one bit. If she didn't know any better, she could have sworn she had turned into—

Luna opened her eyes and stared down at her paws.

—*a dog!*

"Woof!" barked Luna. Her tail thumped the floor. When she turned her head, she saw a jewel-green salamander staring up at her. A salamander with ruby eyes and Claire's grouchy expression.

"Woof!" barked Luna happily. She'd turned into a way cooler animal than Claire!

Claire-the-salamander's forked tongue

darted and she flicked her scaly tail. Luna wagged her floppy tail in return. She tried to feel what kind of dog she was. Part Border collie, she guessed, with maybe some Saint Bernard?

"Excellent, girls," said Grandy. When Luna looked over, she saw that her grandmother also had changed into an animal—an elegant red fox. Grandy the fox made Wilbur the cat look extra shabby.

Luna tried to ask what kind of dog she'd become, but all that came out of her mouth was another cheerful bark.

"Within every witch is the power to transform into a single creature from the animal kingdom," explained foxy Grandy. "The spell is one of the most powerful listed in the Book of Shadows. However, it's listed as a Samaritan Spell. That means it can only be used to help others, and not for your own fun. I guess that's why it's been thirty years since I bothered to be a fox. Now, twins, close your eyes and imagine that you are looking into a mirror. Concentrate."

Luna closed her eyes and pictured herself: brown eyes, six freckles on her nose, bad haircut, and even the little chicken pox scar under her chin.

In a heartbeat, she jumped onto two legs and was Luna-the-girl again.

"Grandy, that's the best spell yet!" she exclaimed. "Outstanding!"

"That's the worst spell ever!" Claire-the-girl sputtered at her side. "Luna gets to be a dog and I'm just a dumb lizard?"

"Salamander," Grandy corrected. "A witch transforms into the animal that best represents her human traits."

"I guess I really am a loyal and trusted companion," Luna noted.

"But I'm not slithery and cold-blooded!" Claire argued.

Grandy looked unconvinced. "If I were you, I'd read up on salamanders." She sniffed. "Interesting. It takes three spices—cumin, coriander, and cardamom—for you to transform, Claire. But not a single spice for you,

Luna. That means that you, Claire, need to memorize the spell, but Luna, it's already here." She tapped her forehead. "Right in your head, in one-star memory files, for whenever you need it."

Now Grandy brushed her hands together and a cigar appeared between her fingers. "Oh, one other thing. If each of you can use this spell to help someone, you'll earn half of your second star."

"Just half?" faltered Luna.

"Everything gets harder as you get better," snapped Grandy. "That's life. But a one-point-five star sorceress is better than a single-starred simpleton."

At the twins' glum faces, Grandy added, "You'll get your spy globes, too. All one-and-a-halfsters do."

Luna exchanged a grin with her twin. Spy globes were cool.

"One last thing," mentioned Grandy as she set the cigar between her teeth. "A Samaritan Spell is about using individual smarts to benefit someone else. So you can't consult your twin when it's time to use the spell. Got it?"

The twins nodded. Got it.

"Good. Time for a smoke, then bed. Nightie-night, twinsies."

With that, Grandy winked one eye and wriggled the opposite ear, which was actually an easy, insta-port spell that jumped her straight from the study and into her bed, her teeth spell-brushed and her clothes spell-changed from satin robes to cotton pajamas.

"A salamander!" Claire shook her head in disbelief once Grandy was gone. "I'm only one up from a beetle or a centipede."

Luna silently agreed. She felt sorry for her twin. "Oh, it's not so bad, Clairsie," she comforted her. "It could have been worse. You could have turned into a cockroach or a rat or a . . ." She yawned. She could not follow her train of thought. "I'm sleepy," she said. "Animal magic takes a lot out of a witch."

Claire let out a giant yawn of her own.

"Stupid spell," she slurred. "I'm sure there was a mix-up. My real, true animal-self is more like a panther, or a wise old owl. It must be some kind of wrong spice or . . ."

Now both of them yawned again. It took all the rest of their energy to wink and wriggle themselves straight to bed.

3

"Don't Bore Us, Dolores!"

DOUBLE DELIGHT WAS BEING filmed two blocks over on Pine Street, so Jill Bundkin allowed the twins and Justin to walk there, as long as they looked both ways before crossing.

Turning onto Pine Street, Claire saw that the whole block had been transformed to look like a fall day. Red and yellow and orange autumn leaves were heaped on the sidewalk, and more colorful leaves had been twisted and tied into the branches of trees that lined the town-house buildings.

Instant October, Claire thought. Wow! Hollywood magic at work!

Movie equipment was set up everywhere. Sawhorses and plastic cones blocked off Pine Street's entrance. Lights, cameras, and folding chairs cluttered its edges. Movie extras in wool sweaters and long pants sat around looking hot and bored. Other men and women in jeans and black T-shirts darted around, speaking on headsets. A crew of T-shirted people was hard at work, sponge-painting red and orange and yellow fall colors onto flat cookie pans of ordinary brown leaves.

"Hey, that looks fun. I bet they'll let me help!" And Justin shot off to pester the painters.

"Yoo-hoo! Gals!" Fluffy waved from behind the snack table that was set up near a big steel trailer.

Fluffy looked extra sparkly today, Claire

noticed. Her denim maternity shirt was studded with jeweled pins shaped like fruit and flowers. Privately, Claire thought it looked like Fluffy had decorated herself with refrigerator magnets.

"Melody is inside, preparing for her next scene," said Fluffy, pointing to the trailer. "She'll be out in a jiffy-pop. I told her all about you two! Ooh, there's Bernardo, the photographer. Howdy, Bern!" Fluffy wriggled her fingers at a skinny bald man who was walking around, aiming and snapping from the large zoom lens camera that hung around his neck.

"You've already met Melody?" Claire squealed. "What's she like? Is she nice? Is she tall or small? Does she look like a big-headed Martian?"

"Naw, sugar, she's just a normal gal," Fluffy answered. "Take a seat, and she'll be out soon."

"Does my headband look okay?" Luna whispered as the girls sat in the folding chairs that Fluffy indicated.

"It hides your nice new haircut I gave you, if that's what you meant," Claire answered, "plus it shows off your pumpkin forehead."

"If I have a pumpkin forehead, that means you have one, too, dummy," Luna retorted.

"Hush, y'all." Fluffy handed the twins each a cup of apple juice and a napkin of graham crackers from the snack table. "Melody will be with us any minute," she said, "so we'll just stay put."

Claire and Luna fell silent. They munched down their crackers and drank their apple juice and stayed put.

And stayed put.

And stayed put some more.

"Look, Justin is painting leaves." Luna pointed to their brother, who was huddled with the crew, a sponge brush in his hand. "I want to paint, too! Are movie sets always this boring? And where is Melody?"

"Oh, don't be so impetuous," said Claire. "Movie stars are known to be temperamental."

"If you keep using those words," warned

Luna, "Melody will think you're a know-it-all nerdburger."

"She will not!"

"Will, too!"

"Will not, double cross my fingers."

"Will too, no crossies count."

"Gals, hush!" Fluffy scolded.

Right then, the door to the trailer opened. Claire jumped from her chair and smiled the warmest-blooded smile that she could muster. Ever since last weekend when she had changed into a salamander, Claire had worried that her human self was cold-blooded as an amphibian. So she had been practicing her warm-blooded smiling.

Now her smile widened. Yes, it was Melody Malady, all right. Wow! And she was walking down the steps directly toward them!

Claire could not wait. She sprinted across the set. "Hi, Melody! My name's Claire Bundkin, and I just want to say that I'm your biggest fan. I think *The Melody Malady Show* is the best thing on television after *Galaxy Murk!*"

Melody smiled as she shook Claire's hand. "Well, thanks!" she said. "I love *Galaxy Murk,* too. Captain Xeno is so cute. Once I got to go on set and sit in his Solar Excelsior. And guess what's inside the space-control compartments? Makeup and hair spray, for his emergency beauty touch-ups!" Melody threw back her head and laughed her throaty, famous laugh.

Claire laughed along in a happy Claire laugh of her own. Was it really possible that Melody Malady was even nicer in person than on television? Amazing!

"What's so funny?" A girl had crept up next to Claire and Melody and was eyeing them suspiciously. She was dressed in cargo shorts and a camouflage vest that was weighted with bulging pockets. Her arms and legs were scabbed and bug-bitten. In one hand, she was carrying a small curved chisel.

The smile dropped off Melody's face.

"Claire," she said, "this is my sister, Dolores."

"Greetings," said Dolores, waving her chisel. "I'm Dolores Gologly. *Gologly* is our family's real last name. It's of Irish descent. As you might have guessed, Malady is a fake stage name of no descent."

"Be quiet, Dolores," said Melody.

"Hi." Claire shook Dolores's free hand, which squeezed back in a granite grip. She turned to Melody. "Cheese and chips! I didn't know you had a sister!"

"We're more than sisters. We're twins," said Dolores.

"Twins!" Claire was dumbfounded.

"Melody is the public, artistic twin and I'm the private, academic twin," said Dolores.

"Dolores, get lost," said Melody. "Go be the silent, invisible twin."

"My twin sister is here, too." Claire looked around. Luna was standing by the snack table, picking grapes out of the fruit salad. "Loon!" she shouted.

Luna approached slowly. Claire made introductions. "Luna loves your show, too!" Claire piped up when Luna forgot to compliment it.

"Really?" Melody smiled. Her teeth were pearly white and perfect.

Luna touched her headband. "Mmm-hmm," she said. She looked over at Dolores. "Whatcha got in your vest pockets?"

"Rocks," Dolores answered. "I collect them. That's why I'm here on this boring movie set, instead of back in Bethesda, Maryland, where we live. The outlying region of Philadelphia is a rich rock resource. If I can get samples of—"

"Don't bore us, Dolores!" snapped Melody. "Aren't we ready for photos or something?"

"Howdy, Melody! I see you've met my twin stepdaughters." Fluffy had appeared with Bernardo the photographer at her side. Every pin on her shirt flashed and glinted in the sun. Claire felt her cheeks flush. Why did

Fluffy have to look so over-sparkly on this important Melody-meeting day?

"Dolores, go back to the trailer with Dad," Melody instructed. "My sister is always under-foot," she explained to Fluffy. "I guess I could get my dad to take her back to the motel."

"Naw, honey, she can stay on set if she wants," said Fluffy. "Maybe we'll do a different spin on the photo shoot. About two sets of twins and—"

"No!" Melody's own cheeks flushed. "Go on, Dolores." Now Melody shoved Dolores semi-gently.

"I didn't want my picture taken, anyhow," said Dolores calmly. "The Fijians believe that the photographic image robs your soul." Turning to Luna, she explained, "See, I'm the academic twin and Melody is the artistic—"

"Beat it!" Melody stamped her foot.

Dolores sighed, turned, and stomped off.

Poor Dolores! thought Claire as she watched her retreat to the trailer. Imagine how awful it would be to have beautiful and talented

Melody Malady for a sister, when all you've got is scabby knees and a vest full of rocks.

It was time for photos. First, Melody's stylist, a guy named Jake, appeared. He combed and spritzed both twins' hair, smoothing Luna's more tightly into its headband. "That haircut'll grow out in no time," Claire heard him whisper to Luna.

Next, Jake spent fifteen minutes taking care of Melody so that every eyelash was in place.

Finally, Bernardo snapped some photographs of Melody with Claire and Luna. He asked them to pretend that they were meeting Melody all over again.

Claire pumped Melody's hand and gave her warmest-blooded smile.

Luna's smile was not quite as warm.

Bernardo clicked and clicked and said, "Fantastic-o, perfect-o!" until he ran out of film.

"Bernie, you're great-o! We've got enough for a darlin' magazine piece," drawled Fluffy.

"I'm hungry," said Melody. "Is my lunch ready?"

"Sorry, Mel," said Bernardo. "Willa says we're about to begin filming."

Melody looked sad. She turned to Claire. "Willa is the movie director, and her word is law. Hey, do you want to hang around and watch?" She looked over at Luna. "You, too, Uma."

"Luna," corrected Luna.

"Wow! I'd love to watch!" said Claire.

"It's too hot to be outside," Luna protested.

Melody pressed a finger to her chin. "You can stay in the trailer with Dolores if you want," she suggested. "It has air-conditioning."

"Okay." Luna said, and walked off.

Claire was aghast. Was Luna crazy? How could she pass up an opportunity to watch a movie being filmed? Crumbs, it wasn't *that* hot!

Or maybe Claire could take the sun better? Like a salamander that breathed through its skin, maintaining a comfortable moisture level in spite of the heat. (The other night, Claire had done some research about salamanders. She found out they had some unusual habits, such as skin breathing.)

"*I* don't think it's too hot, Melody," she said.

"Great!" Melody tugged Claire's arm. "Let's go find you a seat."

Melody might be a big Hollywood star, thought Claire, but she was also *sooo* down to earth. From Jake the stylist to Dina the gaffer to Jorge the key grip, Melody had a smile and kind word for everybody.

That's how I'd be, too, if I were a movie star, Claire decided.

Melody found Claire a seat on one of the high-angle camera stools. Claire climbed up and watched as Willa ordered everyone to places and asked for quiet on the set. In the scene being filmed that day, all Melody had to do was walk across the street and bump into a man exiting a building.

"Take one!" shouted Willa through her

megaphone. Then, "Take two! Take three!"

Melody was wearing winter clothes that must have made her very uncomfortable, but she never complained. She walked and bumped, walked and bumped. Chin in her hands, Claire watched and watched. She could not believe Luna was missing all this action.

After nineteen takes, Willa called, "Okay, that's a wrap. Be back here in two hours."

A few people clapped, relieved. Then Melody took Willa aside and spoke with her, pointing at Claire all the while. Finally, Willa looked over and nodded.

Smiling, Melody ran to Claire.

"Guess what? Willa said a small part could be written into the movie. A part just for you," Melody told her. "Come back tomorrow, Claire, and you can be on the other side of the camera. With me."

"Wow, thanks, Melody!" Claire jumped off her seat and began to hop around from excitement.

Melody Malady, television star, movie star, and now, Claire's costar!

This summer kept getting better and better!

4

Four Point Six Billion

"I'M GOING TO VALLEY FORGE National Park tomorrow," Luna announced that night at the dinner table. She'd had to wait until dessert to speak. Between Claire and Justin's nonstop chatter to their mother—on and on about Melody Malady and her dumb movie— Luna had not been able to squeeze in a word.

Claire and Justin put down their ice-cream spoons. All eyes turned to her.

"Valley Forge Park? *Blech!*" said Claire.

"Why?" asked Justin. "Who with?"

"With *whom?*" asked their mother.

"With Dolores Gologly. Because she invited me. Her dad, Mr. G, is taking us, if that's okay with you, Mom? Mr. G is a geologist, and he's going to teach me about rocks and stuff. He's really nice. Mrs. G is a geologist, too. Right now, she's in Santa Fe doing fieldwork. Dolores says—"

"Wait a minute. Dolores Gologly?" exclaimed Claire. "As in, Dolores, Melody's freaky sister? Yuck! Dolores is a nerd from Planet Absurd!"

"Actually," Luna said, "she's fascinating."

"You're demented, Luna," teased Justin. "Here I've got a paying job as a gofer for the *Double Delight* movie crew, and Claire's got a part in the movie, and you wind up going to Valley Forge National Park. Jeez! We've *all* been to the park for school trips! That's like coming back from a movie set with *homework.*" He and Claire smirked at each other.

"Dolores is a member of the North American Geologists' Organization and the Young Naturalists' Society," explained Luna. "She has read the works of Thoreau, Emerson, and Burroughs. In other words, Dolores is four point six billion times more interesting than Melody, or anyone on her film crew."

This only made Claire and Justin laugh.

"If her brain's half as big as her ego, she's a genius," snorted Claire.

Luna bit her lips and said nothing. Nobody could stop her from being excited about tomorrow.

That night, when Claire and her witch-kitten, Hortense, were sleeping—Claire under the covers and Hortense on top of the covers, at Claire's feet—Luna did something bold. She sneaked into her and Claire's clothes closet and pulled out their Little Book of Shadows.

Although Luna almost never cast spells without her grandmother or her twin, she considered this an emergency.

With her own witch-kitten, Edith, purring at her side, Luna located and memorized the necessary spell on page 557.

She and Edith had to wait until midnight, the witching hour, to cast it. Once her sister was safely snoozing, Luna again crawled out of bed, walked to her bureau, put a hand on each knob of the top drawer, and cast:

"Calcite, fluorite, topaz, quartz!
A modern witch is free of warts.
Steel-tipped hammer, field pouch gear,
My witch-wish is to bring them here!"

From her bathrobe pocket, she pulled out a thin roll of bills and placed it in her sock drawer. It was tough to say good-bye to all that money. For the past five months, Luna had been saving to buy a Sno-Kewl ice shaver so that she could make her own grape or cherry Italian ices. Mmm—refreshing!

"But now I have a better investment, right, Edith?" she whispered.

Edith yawned pointedly. Witch-kittens have growing bones and need their sleep.

The next morning, Luna was up with the sun. Careful not to wake her snoring sister, she opened her dresser drawer. Yes, the money was gone. In its place were a small rock pick, plus a field pouch with a compass button and adjustable belt buckle.

Luna smiled as she gathered up her new geologist's tools. There were times when being a one-star witch was very convenient!

At eight o' clock, Mr. Gologly's car pulled up to the Bundkins' town house.

"Glad you're prompt, Luna! Now we have an early start on the day," said Mr. G as Luna climbed into the backseat with Dolores.

"A day away from our motel rooms and the dumb *Double Delight* set," added Dolores.

"Hey, come on. Your sister is going to make a great movie, Dolores," chided Mr. G. "We need to show family support."

Dolores breathed out hard through her nose in answer.

Mr. G was nice, thought Luna. He was a regular dad, who, like Dolores, was on the brainy side. In fact, in looks and personality, Mr. G seemed to be lots more like Dolores than his famous daughter.

"What I really dig about Valley Forge Park are its quartz grains," proclaimed Mr. G as he drove into the visitor parking lot, which was already filling up with tour buses. "We'll find some super samples along Mount Misery and Mount Joy. They're the topographic highlights of the park. Heck, I haven't seen those mountains since Mrs. G's and my school days."

Luna patted her field pouch, which fit snugly around her waist. Soon it would be filled with rock samples. Yesterday, Dolores had informed her all about rocks.

"A map of the earth's past" Dolores had said. She went on to explain that some rocks had been created by ancient volcanoes, others by continent collisions and shifting icebergs. "But no rock is ever boring!" Dolores explained. Each one, she said, had its own ancient history.

After Mr. G collected their day permits from the information booth, they sprang through the gates and into the park. Luna stretched her arms into the wide, open space. Beautiful!

Last fall, her teacher, Mrs. Sanchez, had taken the entire fifth grade on a science field trip to this very park. All Luna could remember of that trip was that she had suffered a stomach cramp from eating her egg salad sandwich too fast, and that Claire accidentally had left on the bus the postcards they had bought at the Valley Forge Log Cabin gift shop.

It had not been a good day.

Today Luna saw the park in a new light. Bursting with rock treasures.

"This park is gorgeous!" Dolores brandished her chisel. "Of course, Melody would hate it. She hates the Great Outdoors."

"Dolores, is it hard to have a famous sister?" Luna asked. "Do you ever get jealous?"

"No," Dolores answered quickly. "But. Sometimes it's, um, *inconvenient*. Like we can't even go to the mall or the movies, because everyone wants Melody's autograph and stuff. That's all going to change, though," Dolores added, her chin jutting upward. "Not to brag, but because of my straight-As in science, my school has sponsored me as this year's sixth-grade entry to the Bethesda State Fair. I'm going to make my mark on the world by collecting the widest variety of rock samples ever gathered on the northeastern North American coast."

"Crumbs! Then you'll be famous, too!" exclaimed Luna.

"Well, yes, but only in academic circles," Dolores admitted.

The morning passed quickly. Mr. G and Dolores showed Luna how to find rocks from the least-weathered outcroppings. As the girls measured and chipped, Mr. G told the history of Valley Forge. In geology terms, the park was 525 million years old. Amazing!

Luna also enjoyed listening to Mr. G reel

off the names of Valley Forge's rocks.

Dolomite, siltstone, limestone, sandstone, and *shale.*

Sedimentary, igneous, and *metamorphic.*

Magma and *lava.*

Poor Claire, thought Luna. Claire loved-loved-loved exotic words.

Claire was missing everything!

It was midway down the side of Mount Misery that Dolores made the discovery. Half hidden along the edge of Mount Misery's basin and rising up steeply from a thin, shallow stream was the entrance to a cave.

"Wow!" Luna peered inside. It was too dark to see much. "Do you think we can go in?"

"There's no sign saying we can't," Dolores observed.

"What about your dad? He probably won't let us." Dolores and Luna both looked up to where Mr. G was standing at the top of the mountain. Out of earshot, he was examining some rust-stained sedimentary rock.

"We'll only be a minute. I bet some of the

deposits in this cave are limestone," said Dolores. "In limestone, you can find fossils of trilobites and brachiopods."

Fossils! That did it. "Let's go!" said Luna

The cave was icy and smelled like mold. After a few steps inside, Luna could not even see her feet. She shivered.

From outside, Mr. G called both girls' names.

"Coming, coming." Dolores clicked on and shined her pocket flashlight on the slimy, dripping walls. "Limestone, as I suspected." She took out her chisel. She picked and chipped.

Luna stood in place. "It's too dark to find a fossil," she said. Her voice bounced off the wall in worried echoes. "My field pouch is heavy enough."

"For fossils, we need to go deeper," suggested Dolores. "This cave tunnels on for a while. I want to collect more samples for my science fair project."

Mr. G called the girls' names again.

"I think we've seen enough," said Luna. "Let's go, Dolores."

"If you go, then I have to go," Dolores complained. "The rules of geology are stay with your buddy."

For the third time, Mr. G called them. His voice sounded far away, as if he were searching in the wrong direction.

"That's it! See ya!" Luna ducked out of the cave. A minute later, Dolores appeared. Together, they bounded up the side of the mountain toward Mr. G.

Relief filled his face when he saw them. "Cripes. Where *were* you girls?"

"No place special," Luna said. She and Dolores exchanged small smiles. The cave was a secret place.

"Let's go explore the southern side of the park," said Mr. G. "And then lunch!"

"Okay!" the girls agreed.

By the time they stopped at the Valley Forge Inn for a very late feast, Luna was exhausted. Rocks, mountains, streams, a secret cave—what a day!

Sitting at one of the outdoor tables of the inn's porch, watching the sun glaze the treetops with late afternoon light, Luna realized something.

"I am going to become a geologist when I grow up," she announced. "Or a detective. I love-love-love to uncover hidden layers."

"Well, heck, that's wonderful, Luna," said Mr. G. He raised his glass of lemonade. "Three cheers to you!"

Then Luna and Dolores raised their glasses, too, and clinked them.

"Not to brag," said Dolores, "but I knew I would be a geologist when I was in second grade. Then again, I'm very advanced for my age."

5
Claire La Dare

*T*HAT MORNING AFTER HER sister had left for Valley Forge Park, Claire cast a private spell of her own.

It was not a major spell. It was actually a teensy "tidy-up" spell that Claire had memorized last year. She memorized it because she used it a lot.

Here's how it worked.

After taking a shower, wrap your towel

tight around you, tucking it in the front. Next, standing on the bath mat, close your eyes and *squeeeeze* the water from your hair, letting it *drip, drip, drip* until the bath mat is so squelchy that someone might yell at you about it.

Then chant:

Polish, press, button, comb, tie, clean, tidy ME!

And, presto!

If Claire ended up putting on her underwear inside out, or if she forgot to brush her hair in the back, or if her buttons were buttoned wrong or her zips half zipped, the tidy-up spell would automatically fix all that, so she looked neat as a new shoe.

Claire reserved the spell for special occasions. Like the first day of school. Or Thanksgiving. Or whenever she went to Freedom Skate.

Or today. Today was a special occasion, definitely! Because today was when she, Claire

Bundkin, might become a movie star.

"A *celebrity*," she said to Hortense. Claire loved-loved-loved that word. It reminded her of a long, cool piece of celery with a bright light shining on it.

Hortense sighed and mewed sadly. She didn't like the bath mat to be wet, because that was where she took her midmorning naps.

Maybe I've always known I'd be a movie star, Claire mused as she and Justin hurried to Pine Street later that morning. Justin was wearing the new T-shirt the crew had given him yesterday in exchange for his leaf-painting work. On its front were printed the words DOUBLE DELIGHT. On the back was printed FILM CREW. From the way he was strutting, Claire had a feeling this was Justin's new favorite shirt.

"Hey, Claire, how did you get your sandals so clean?" Justin asked. "Yesterday I thought I saw you step in paint."

"These are Luna's sandals," Claire lied—

because of course the tidy-up spell had insta-scraped the paint off Claire's sandals.

Melody was in her trailer. She wore the same heavy winter clothes as the day before.

"Claire, guess what? The writers made you a part. You're going to be a girl at the table next to mine in the outdoor café scene!" Melody squealed. "I'm at one table drinking apple cider, and you're at another table, and you look over at me and say, 'Mom, I want some hot apple cider!'"

"Mom, I want some hot apple cider!" Claire jumped up and down.

"We're about the same size, so wardrobe said you should wear this. It's from my closet." Melody handed Claire a thick sweater and long pants and a parka. "Ugh! Now you'll know how I feel. You can use my dressing room to change. It's in the back."

"Okay!" Claire grinned. Melody's own dressing room! Wow!

The dressing room was the size of a post-card. Claire kept bumping her funny bone into the wall. When she came out, she felt scratchy and thick.

"Hurry!" urged Melody. "Willa has called us to places."

At the end of the Pine Street, a pretend café with tables, chairs, and an outdoor fountain had been set up.

Claire spied Justin with the rest of the crew, moving café tables and chairs into different groupings on Willa's instruction. Claire gave him a movie star-ish wave, but he didn't notice.

Willa steered Claire to a café table. Two other extras, a man and woman in winter-clothes costumes, were already sitting there. They were drinking bottled water and fanning themselves with their hands.

"I guess we're your parents," said the woman with a sniff, looking Claire up and down.

The man shrugged and said nothing.

"This is so awesome!" Claire exclaimed. "I hope this movie is a blockbuster and everyone at school sees me and is jealous!"

"It sure better be a blockbuster," said the woman. "Melody needs one."

"Yeah, I heard they were pulling the plug on her show," said the man.

The Melody Malady Show, canceled? Claire frowned. "That's impossible," she said. "It's the second-best show on television."

"Ratings are down," said the man. "Melody's too old. She used to be cute, but now, eh. She's so-so."

"I never saw her show," said the woman, "but I heard it's a load of garbage."

"No way, it's great!" Claire protested. How dare they! She salamander-stared hard at the man and woman. (She had read that salamanders could stare at the same object for hours without blinking.) "Don't talk against Melody. She's my friend."

"Sorry, kid, but that's what I heard," said the woman.

The café scene dragged all morning. Willa called for take after take.

By the twenty-eighth time, Claire was tired of saying, "Mom, I want some hot apple cider!"

By the fiftieth take, sweat was prickling beneath Claire's wool clothes, and her mouth was dry as lint.

Hot apple cider was the last thing she wanted.

"Okay, perfect," called Willa. "That's a wrap."

"Finally!" croaked Claire.

Melody laughed. "Think how I feel! I never drank so much apple cider in my life. They've set up lunch in my trailer. Let's peel off these clothes and get some grub!"

Only the grub turned out to be green salad and protein shakes.

"Yick!" said Claire. "Bring on the peanut-butter-and-jelly sandwiches! Bring on the ice-cream sandwiches! I'm hungry!"

"Sorry. It's the studio's orders," Melody explained sadly. "All they serve are these shakes and salads. Day after day."

"Being a movie star is hard work, huh?" said Claire through a mouthful of salad.

Melody nodded. "And everyone expects me to be cheerful and nice all the time. As soon as I do one thing wrong—like if I complain about retakes or say I'm tired—the rumors start that I'm a spoiled brat."

"But it must be fun-fun-fun to be famous!" said Claire. "You get to live half the year in Hollywood and you don't do chores."

"I guess," said Melody.

"I want to be famous, too," Claire announced. "I want to have a million-dollar smile and charm to spare, like they write about movie stars in those movie magazines. I want to be a celebrity!"

"You do?"

"Sure. Doesn't everybody?"

Melody looked puzzled. "I never had a choice. When I was six months old, I was discovered at the supermarket by a talent scout. One week later I was the Hush-a-bye Bassinet Baby. So I don't know any different."

"Well, I don't know any different than being *un*famous," said Claire. "But I'm sure I want to be a star! Hey, will you teach me how, Melody?"

"How to be star? Gee, I don't know. But I think the first step," said Melody, "is wardrobe."

"Wardrobe?" Claire looked down at the striped T-shirt and shorts she was wearing. They used to be red, but hundreds of trips through the wash had faded them to the color of raspberry sherbet.

"You know, eye-catching clothes." Melody jumped to her closet. She pulled out a span-gled gold shirt and gold hat with a jaunty feather. "I wore this on the season finale of my show," she said. "You can have it."

"I remember that outfit!" Claire pulled the gold shirt over her striped one and set the feathered hat on her head. "Thanks, Melody." Already, she felt shiny and slightly different from her unfamous Claire self.

"Second step," said Melody, her finger pressed to her chin. "I think you need to change your name to something *starrier*."

"Like—Bonnie-Blue Bundkin?" Claire

had always wished her parents had named her Bonnie-Blue.

"No, no, no. Claire is a nice name. It's the last part where I'd put more snap." Melody tipped her head, studying Claire. "Maybe to . . . Claire Clarinet? Or Claire Éclair? Or Claire Airedale?"

Claire sipped her extremely *eww* protein shake and thought. "How about . . . Claire La Dare?"

Melody snapped her fingers. "Exactly!"

"Claire La Dare." Claire said it again, her new celebrity name.

"Gosh, Claire, I'm really happy that we met," said Melody. "There aren't many people my age who are working in Hollywood, and back in Bethesda, I'm never in school long enough to make a real friend."

"You've got to be kidding! Everyone and anyone in Bethesda, or Hollywood, or the whole U.S. of A. wants to be your friend, Melody!" said Claire.

"Everyone might, but nobody *is*," said Melody.

And for a moment, Melody Malady looked sad.

Only for a moment, though.

Then her TV-perfect Melody face switched back on, million-dollar smile, dimples, and all.

6
Sister Scrap Heap

LUNA LOVED-LOVED-LOVED the sixty-eight rocks in her brand-new rock collection. She had borrowed Dolores's Li'l Miner Rock Cleaner and Dolores's Li'l Miner Rock Polisher to scrub and shine every single one.

When she was finished cleaning and polishing, Luna set her varnished rocks in a glinting row on her windowsill, from her largest chunk of shale all the way down to her tiniest potassium pebble.

"I'm going to find a fair, or some kind of contest around Philadelphia and enter my rocks in it," she said to Claire as she gave her rock garden a final overview. "Do you think my rocks could win a prize?"

The twins were up in their bedroom, where they were supposed to be making back-to-school supply lists for their mother.

Claire was standing in front of the closet full-length mirror. She was wearing her new gold shirt and feathered hat and admiring herself.

"Do you think my rocks could win a prize?" Luna repeated.

Claire mumbled something under her breath.

"What did you say?"

"Nothing."

Luna flushed. "It sounded like you said, 'Who cares, geolo-geek.' You better stop calling me that, Claire. It's rude." And it hurt her feelings. Luna did not say that part.

"I didn't call you geolo-geek," Claire scoffed. "Crumbs, why do you have to be so sensitive all the time about every single thing?"

Luna bit her lips and did not answer. These past few days, she felt as if something had happened to her sister. It was as if Claire had been stolen away and replaced by a zombietron. Like the ones on *Galaxy Murk*. The zombietron *looked* like Claire and *sounded* like Claire, but all that came out of her mouth were rude, un-Claire-ish comments.

"Melody has changed you," Luna decided to speak what had been on her mind for a little while now. "And yesterday Dolores and I agreed that neither of you are much fun to be around when you get together."

"Ha. You're just jealous because I'm friends with the movie star twin, and you got the rock star twin." Claire smirked at her own joke.

"I am *not* jealous," Luna protested. "Dolores is fantastic. Every day this week we've done something cool with Mr. G. We've been to Olde City and the Planetarium and the Franklin Institute."

"Oh, Loon, tons of people go to the Franklin Institute. But how many people can watch a real-live movie being made? A movie where I happen to have a small, but important, supporting role," Claire added.

Luna frowned. "When we're out at Licks 'n' Sticks with Dad and Fluffy tomorrow night, you and Melody had better be nice to Dolores and me."

"I'll be however I want," said Claire. "I'm Claire La Dare."

"Claire La Dare? What are you talking about? And, by the way, have you been casting that tidy-up spell on yourself?" Luna shook her finger. "Your hair looks too combed. Plus it has a perfect, no-mistakes spell-smell to it."

"How would you know, Loon?" Claire pointed a finger back. "You couldn't smell your way out of a wet sock."

Luna blinked. She was touchy about her

bad sense of smell. She could not believe that Claire was teasing her for it.

"Claire, telephone!" called Justin from behind the door. "It's you-know-who!"

"Coming! Coming!" Claire yelled.

Luna watched as her zombietron sister skipped off to take Melody's call. Melody called every night. For a big-shot television star, she sure seemed lonely.

Then Luna stood and walked over to Claire's side of their room, which was covered in glossy autographed publicity photos of Melody. In order to find space for the new photos, Claire had pulled down some of her old ones.

School pictures. Camp pictures.

Worse, Claire had pulled down some twin pictures.

Luna picked up a photograph of herself and Claire that her sister had tossed in a scrap heap on her bedside table. The photograph had been taken this past spring, at their father's wedding to Fluffy. That same afternoon that the twins had become one-star witches and received their witch-kittens.

A special day, when they had hooked pinkies and danced the hula.

Yesterday, Luna confided to Claire all about the secret cave in Valley Forge Park. In return, Claire confided to Luna that she'd taught their special pinkie-hook to Melody Malady.

And she hadn't even asked Luna's permission first!

"I gave Claire a secret, and Claire gave away a secret," Luna told Edith mournfully. "That doesn't seem fair, does it? All it took was one week, and now it's like Claire wants to be identical twins with Melody instead of me."

Her kitten, understanding humanspeak, purred soothingly. Luna sat on the rug and gathered Edith into her arms. Then, on second thought, she called Hortense, too. "Here, kitty. Come here, Hort."

Hortense jumped off the foot of Claire's

bed and leaped to the comfort of Luna's arms. Claire had not been giving Hortense much attention this week. All of Claire's time and energy was going straight to Melody.

Luna snuggled both kittens into her lap.

"How can I compete if Claire wants to be stuck like glue to superstar Melody?" asked Luna. "Claire and I don't even *look* identical anymore, ever since she gave me this bad haircut."

Edith and Hortense purred a soft rumble of sympathy.

"I don't want to say it," Luna spoke softly, "but I'll be glad when Melody finishes up her movie and goes home. I really do like Dolores, but I'd rather have my own sister back."

But she had a sad hunch that right now, Claire did not share this feeling.

The next night, as a special almost-back-to-school treat, Fluffy and their father were taking Justin and Luna and Claire and Dolores and Melody out for dinner.

"Licks 'n' Sticks is our favorite family

restaurant," explained Luna as they all scrambled out of the car.

"Is the food low in calories?" asked Melody.

"Yeah, is it?" asked Claire. She was wearing her gold shirt and gold feathered hat and a pair of Melody's dark wraparound sunglasses. She looked very silly, in Luna's opinion.

"Aw, you won't care 'bout calories when the food's so good!" said Fluffy.

"I'm getting a hot fudge sundae," said Dolores. "People are usually confused about calorie intake, especially considering the statistics—"

"Oh, blah-blah-blah, Dolores!" snapped Melody.

For all her niceness to everyone else, Luna thought, Melody was tough on her own twin. Was this the same attitude that had rubbed off on Claire?

The hostess sat Luna, Dolores, Fluffy, Melody, Claire, Justin, and their dad in their usual half-circle booth.

"Wow, we're a doggone crowd tonight!" exclaimed Fluffy. She was wearing her special-occasion red-fringed maternity cowgirl pantsuit with the horseshoe-buckle belt.

"Can I get two hot dog sticks and no vegetable sticks?" asked Justin as he opened his menu.

"Can I get some carrot sticks and no dessert?" asked Claire, with a look over at Melody.

"Actually, I want the deep-fried dumpling sticks and a hot fudge sundae," said Melody. "Since I'm not on the movie set, I can eat what I want."

"Oh, yeah, me, too," Claire agreed.

Luna noticed that at other booths and tables, heads were beginning to turn and people were whispering. At first Luna thought it was because of Fluffy's remarkable cowgirl clothes. Then she realized it was on account of Melody Malady.

"Please, just ignore them," said Melody. She was using her menu to shield her face.

"Okay." Their father put on his best newspaper reporter voice. "So, everybody, who is looking forward to the start of school?"

"Hi!" A father and daughter had bounced up to their booth. "Aren't you Melody Malady? You're fantastic! What a singer! What a dancer! Can we get your autograph?"

"Sure." Melody smiled, wrote her name on a napkin, and handed it over.

"Bye, now, y'all!" said Fluffy, waving them off. She turned to Melody and said, "Some folks have red-hot-poker nerve! Interrupting us in the middle of dinner like that."

Unfortunately, no sooner had the father and daughter left, than it happened again.

"We're totally too old for your show, and we think it's kinda stupid, but we want your autograph anyway," said a teenaged couple who had sidled up to Melody from the next booth over.

They thrust a pen and piece of paper in front of Melody.

Melody's TV-perfect expression stayed

sweetly in place as she nodded and signed away.

Poor Melody, thought Luna, having to be polite even though the teenagers were so impolite to her. Luna knew she sometimes tended to feel jealous of Melody. First for being a star, and also for hogging up Claire's attention. But now Luna felt a *pinch* sorry for Melody Malady.

After all, it couldn't be much fun for a person to be so perfect-perfect-perfect in public all the time.

"Do you want my autograph, too?" Claire asked the teenagers. "I'm in Melody's next big feature movie. It might be my breakout movie star role."

"Uh, okay." The teenagers looked at Claire skeptically.

Talk about red-hot-poker nerve, thought Luna. She watched as her sister wrote the name *Claire La Dare* in giant letters next to Melody's. Claire's nose pressed close to the page.

"What's wrong with that girl's eyes?" one of the teenagers whispered.

Justin laughed. "Yo, Madame La Dare, I think that's a signal that you should take off your sunglasses!" he said. "You can't even see through them!"

"Be quiet, Justin," muttered Claire, but she pushed her sunglasses up onto her hat.

"Come on, gang. Time to order," said their father.

Just as they turned back to their menus, yet another group, this time a family of a mother, a father, and two squawking kids presented themselves for Melody's autograph. "Please-please-please-please-please!" they yelped.

"Do you want my autograph? I'm also in Melody's movie," said Claire.

"Nah. We don't recognize you," said one of the kids. "Let's go." And they moved off.

At that, Justin laughed outright, but Luna saw that her twin sister was starting to get her pointy look. When things were not going Claire's way, every edge of her body—elbows, nose, shoulder blades—seemed to sharpen and turn brittle as glass.

Justin did not seem to notice. He kept right on teasing.

"Madame La Dare, you should have left your Halloween costume at home," Justin said.

"For your information, this shirt and hat belong to Melody, and she wore them on the season finale of her show," Claire told Justin. "It's a famous outfit."

"Famous on a famous person, maybe." Justin snickered. "But dumb on a regular person."

"I'm not regular!" cried Claire.

"Regular-regular-reg·u·lar—*Claire*," crowed Justin.

"Cut it *out!* At least I'm not dressed up like a cowgirl!"

Quiet dropped over the table. Out of the corner of her eye, Luna caught a glimpse of Fluffy's hurt, surprised face.

Poor Fluffy! What a terrible thing for Claire to say!

Luna could tell Claire regretted it, too. She blinked, as if shocked by her own words.

"I guess I am looking kinda cowgirly tonight," said Fluffy, plucking at her fringed sleeve. "Maybe the horseshoe belt was overdoing it." She gave an embarrassed-sounding laugh.

"Claire, that kind of rudeness is unacceptable," said their father. "Apologize to Fluffy."

"I'm sorry, Fluffy," said Claire. "I didn't mean it."

"Honey, it's nothing," said Fluffy. She sounded sincere, but she continued to look embarrassed.

Nice going, Claire La Dare, thought Luna.

When Claire looked across the table, silently imploring her twin's help, Luna quickly averted her eyes to her menu.

Claire would have to take care of this one on her own.

7
Salamander Eye Spy

THAT NIGHT, CLAIRE COULD not sleep. So many people were upset with her.

Her dad! Luna! Fluffy!

Even Hortense was mad at her! Tonight, her very own kitten was curled into a small ball of fur at the foot of Luna's bed, next to Edith. Claire had coaxed and called, but her kitten wouldn't jump over. Holding a witch-kitten grudge, Claire figured, because she had not been getting enough attention.

But it was what she had done to Fluffy, that made Claire feel most ashamed.

Why had she blurted that rude remark about Fluffy's cowgirl pantsuit? Crumbs, she hadn't meant to! It was only that Justin had been teasing her too much. When Claire was around Melody, she did not like to feel childish and uncool. The way a big brother or a too-colorfully dressed stepmother could make her feel.

Maybe that's what Luna had meant when she'd said Melody brought out the worst in her.

"Do you think Fluffy truly accepted my apology?" Claire had asked Luna as they settled down for bed.

"Actually, I think you need to do better than apologize," Luna had answered in her frostiest, thirteen-minutes-older-sister voice. "That was an awful thing to say to our not-even-wicked stepmother, Clairsie."

Warthogs and waffle irons! thought Claire. Why did Luna have to make her feel even more miserable? But in her heart, Claire knew her twin was right.

All night, Claire shifted and kicked the covers. How could she make it up to Fluffy? What could she do that was better than saying sorry?

By the next morning, Claire had come up with a plan. She would use her salamander trick to go spy on Fluffy. Then maybe she could learn some kind of special gift to get her. A Good Samaritan gift. That would be even better than a regular apology.

As soon as she finished her breakfast of Oaty-oats cereal and blueberries, Claire telephoned Melody.

"What time is it?" Melody yawned.

"Early. Listen, Melody, I can't come to the set today," said Claire.

"But we're shooting the kidnapping scene! And there's only three days left until the movie's done!" wailed Melody. "I thought we could spend every day together until I have to go back home."

"Me, too," said Claire, "but something urgent came up." Over the phone, Claire could sense Melody's disappointment. "I'll see you tomorrow. Promise."

She clicked off. Although it was too-too-too fun to be friends with a celebrity, a tiny corner of Claire figured that she would be, oh, just a *pinch* relieved when Melody's movie was finished. It took a lot of energy to be Melody Malady's only friend in the whole world.

Claire looked at her wristwatch. She did not have a lot of time. She needed to catch the morning bus to Chestnut Condominiums, pronto.

She quickly showered and dressed and— careful not to wake Luna—flipped through their Little Book of Shadows and memorized the spell. In the kitchen, she carefully spooned the necessary spices into three separate paper twist packets. She did not want to mess up anything.

The dew was soft on the grass and the sun was shining bright but not hot by the time

Claire hopped off the local bus and trekked the quarter mile to Chestnut Condominiums, where her father and Fluffy lived. She was relieved to see that the morning paper was still folded on the doorstep.

Standing on the welcome mat, Claire glanced right and left, unwrapped and sprinkled the spices over her head, then chanted:

"*Cumin, cardamom, coriander,*
Eye of spying salamander,
Animalia kingdom, Amphibia class,
Wriggling webbed toes, touch the grass."

She closed her eyes and let the spell do its work.

First came a chill in her blood. Then a shrinking in her ears, throat, and legs, which was soon followed by a lengthening in her tailbone.

When she opened her bulging eyes, the transformation was complete.

Claire the bottle-green, ruby-eyed, three-inch-long salamander scurried up the side of the wall.

For a few minutes, Claire-the-salamander perched unblinking and basking in the sun's warmth until her father opened the front door. When he bent to retrieve the paper, Claire scurried inside.

In the kitchen, Fluffy was already awake and ready for work. She was slumped at the kitchen table, drinking tea. She was talking, but Claire could not understand a word.

"Mmmmm mmmm mmmm!" said Fluffy.

Claire could feel in her feet and tail the tremors of Fluffy's voice. What was she saying?

Then Claire remembered. Salamanders don't have ears!

Oh, no! How will I be able to eavesdrop, Claire thought, and how can I find out what kind of special gift to get Fluffy, if I can't even hear what she says?

Claire slithered up the leg of Fluffy's chair and leaped onto her suit jacket that was draped over the chair back. She arranged herself between a gold and silver dragonfly pin and a pink pineapple pin. She curled her tail prettily. At least Claire-the-salamander-pin was a perfect disguise, hiding right out in the open with Fluffy's other jewelry!

When Fluffy stood and slid on her suit jacket, she was still talking.

"Mmm hmmm rmmm." Fluffy frowned and pointed to her feet and shook her head at Claire's father.

"Hmm mmmrrrmrrr," said Claire's father. He seemed troubled as he wagged his head back at her.

But Claire could not figure out why Fluffy was so upset. She looked okay from Claire's view, perched high on her jacket lapel and partly concealed by a wave of Fluffy's hair (that smelled nice, like spearmint chewing gum).

As Fluffy and her father walked out to the car, Claire dug in her clawless toes and kept still. She hoped that she blended in with the rest of Fluffy's colorful accessories. She did not need her father's observant newspaper reporter's eye singling her out.

Except for the vibration of Fluffy's weary sighing, the car ride into Philadelphia was smooth. Claire stared out the window and tried not to think about eating the tiny, but very yummy-looking fruit fly that had landed on the window glass.

Hold off until you can eat real food, she told herself. Fruit flies probably aren't fruit-flavored.

When they got to Center City, her father dropped off Fluffy with a kiss.

Claire enjoyed riding the elevator with Fluffy, up-up-up to the forty-fourth floor where the magazine offices of *Philadelphia Now!* were located.

"Rrr-rrr-rrr!" Fluffy called to the receptionist, who waved.

As she moved down the halls, Fluffy stopped and chatted with her other co-workers.

This is fun, Claire thought. If only I could

hear what was going on!

Fluffy made herself a cup of tea in the employee kitchen and went into her office. She turned on her computer and her desk lamp. Then she eased herself into her desk chair. Claire watched intently as Fluffy took out a piece of notepaper and wrote:

marshmallows

soy butter

pickles

pistachio bread

bedroom slippers, size 10 double extra wide

Aha! Claire thought.

Then Fluffy put down her pen and pulled off her suit jacket. Claire's tail curled tight around the pineapple pin for balance as Fluffy tossed the jacket on a coat hook above a filing cabinet.

"Mmmm!" Suddenly, Fluffy stood up from her chair and glanced at her watch. "Mrrmrmr rrmrrmr." She hurried from the office, shutting the door.

Claire's small salamander heart was beating fast. No time to lose.

She dropped off Fluffy's jacket, landing on all fours on the filing cabinet.

Quickly, to undo the spell, Claire closed her eyes and imagined that she was looking into a mirror.

Brown hair, warm-blooded smile, six freckles on the tip of her nose.

In the next moment, Claire-the-salamander was transformed back to Claire-the-girl again.

She slid off the filing cabinet and pocketed Fluffy's list. Now to sneak out of here. She made a couple of wrong turns before she found the receptionist area.

"Hey, you!" called the receptionist.

Oh, no. Caught! Claire turned. "Yes?"

"Are you Coffee Bean's delivery kid?"

"Uh, that's right," Claire answered with a gulp.

"Come here, then."

Reluctantly, Claire approached his desk.

"Get me a large iced vanilla coffee." The

receptionist thrust some money into Claire's hand. "And fast!"

Bewildered, Claire nodded, took the money, and dashed to the elevator just as it *pinged* and the door opened.

Once safe outside, she sprinted the nine blocks home.

Luckily, her mom was at work, and nobody else was there to ask questions. In her bedroom, Claire shook out her savings from her shoe-box bank. She had been planning to buy herself some voice and dance lessons, in order to polish her movie-star qualities.

"But now I have a better investment, right, Horty?"

Her kitten yawned, uninterested. Still holding a grudge, Claire figured.

After one bus stop to the grocery store, Claire used her savings to buy the items on Fluffy's list. Marshmallows, soy butter, pickles, pistachio bread. She also bought some catnip for Edith and Hortense.

The Bed & Beauty store was a few blocks over. Claire had a little trouble finding double extra-wide, size-ten slippers. But there was one more pair left in the back.

Claire had more trouble saying farewell to the rest of her money.

She even remembered the receptionist's vanilla iced coffee, since Coffee Bean was right across the street from Fluffy's work building. The line was long, though, and the cup was hard to balance in one hand.

Weighted with bags, Claire returned to the *Philadelphia Now!* offices.

She was starting to feel very hot.

And sweaty. And tired. And a little depressed.

Fluffy probably wasn't even mad about the cowgirl remark, thought Claire. Why had she gone and spent her whole morning and all her money on this gigantic apology?

On the forty-fourth floor, Claire smacked down the drink in front of the receptionist.

"Your change is my tip," she told him.

Then she marched down the hall to Fluffy's office and opened the door without knocking.

"Claire? What are you doin' here, sugar?" Fluffy's voice was friendly.

Aha! Luna had been wrong! Fluffy was not upset with her, after all!

Claire dropped her bags.

"I got you some special food," she said, "because I felt bad about what I said last night about your cowgirl clothes."

Then Claire dropped down onto the carpet and burst into tears. All her celebrity-lesson money, gone!

"Aw, I know you didn't mean what you said last night." Fluffy stood and walked over from her desk. She eased herself down on the carpet to sit next to Claire. "You shouldn't have taken such trouble and expense," Fluffy soothed.

Which only made Claire cry harder. She really shouldn't have!

Fluffy peeped in the bags. "Oh, golly. My favorite foods. You even got me a pair of slippers?" She shook her head wonderingly. "You must be a mind reader. I was just telling your daddy this morning how my feet had stretched out of my old pair. I think carrying this extra weight has kinda widened 'em out." She patted the bump that was Ubiquitous. "But how did you know?"

"I had a hunch." Claire sniffled. She wished she could stop crying. It did not seem very noble.

"Claire, sugar, I hope you don't feel like you gotta treat me like a guest, and buy me a present every time you think you've said the wrong thing. I'm family now."

"I know," said Claire, but she realized that she did not exactly know.

Fluffy still looked concerned. "'Cause I can be teased and tease back, same as you. Okay?"

"Okay," sniffled Claire. Teasing Fluffy. That would be weird.

"But I gotta also say, since you went and did it, I think your gifts are awful nice." Fluffy placed a hand on each of Claire's shoulders. Claire looked up into Fluffy's wide eyes. "You want to know why?"

"Why?" Claire sniffled again.

"Well, let me tell you, I have been havin' just a terrible thundercloud morning! And *nothing* is better when you're having a thundercloud morning than to feel some unexpected sunshine. Which is what you are today, Claire. Unexpected sunshine."

And Fluffy leaned over and hugged her, hard.

Crumbs, thought Claire, wiping her eyes on Fluffy's jacket lapel where Claire-the-salamander had perched only a couple of hours ago. It was kind of nice to be somebody's unexpected sunshine.

It made Claire feel shiny and golden, but not in a celebrity way. In a special Claire-ish way, which she figured was maybe just as good.

8

Timbuctu to the Rescue

MELODY MALADY'S MOVIE was nearly finished.

"Tomorrow they're filming the parachuting scene," Justin informed Luna, Claire, and their mother while they were gathered at the table for dinner. "It's gonna be the best part of *Double Delight*. And the only reason to see it, in my book."

"Melody gets to parachute off a ledge

onto a trampoline," Claire explained. "Of course, you won't see the ledge and trampoline in the movie. It'll look like she used her secret moon-jumping boots. It's gonna be extra-extra-cool!"

"Sounds spectacular," said their mother.

"I won't be there," said Luna, wiping her mouth with her napkin. "Dolores and I have better plans. We're going to see the Philadelphia Rare Flower Show. Mr. G is taking us."

"That also sounds spectacular, Luna," said their mother.

"Ugh!" said Justin.

"Boring!" said Claire.

They made faces at each other.

Luna did not care. She was just happy that she and Dolores weren't spending the day chipping for rock samples. Dolores was a little too nuts for rocks, Luna had decided. She wanted to win that science fair in Bethesda like crazy. She talked about it all the time.

Maybe too much of the time.

Luna really liked rocks, too, but lately she had realized that she didn't love-love-love them. She was happy enough with her windowsill rock garden. She was not even sure that she wanted to be a geologist anymore.

The other night, she had watched a television documentary about lighthouses, and now she thought she might make a good lighthouse keeper. That would be a romantic job. She liked to picture a midnight sea and a cleft-chinned captain, his ship saved by Luna's brave and steadfast light!

But Luna had decided not to tell Dolores that she didn't care so much about rocks anymore. Dolores might take it too personally.

The next morning, Justin, Luna, and Claire made their last trip to Pine Street to the *Double Delight* set. Justin strutted ahead.

"See-ya, wouldn't wanna be-ya," he called, and shot off.

"Even when Justin is at his worst, tease-wise, he's nicer to us than Melody is to Dolores," Luna said. "It's strange. Melody is so sweet to everyone else, but not to her own sister."

"Well, you have to admit," said Claire, "Dolores is a freak from Planet Bleak."

"*I* think Dolores is great. I'll be sad when she goes home," said Luna.

"I'll be sad when Melody leaves," said Claire. "It's not every day I get to be best friends with a movie star."

Luna did not answer. She thought that *she* was Claire's best friend. But maybe being a twin didn't automatically make you a *best*. After all, Melody and Dolores weren't best friends. They weren't even friendly.

Still, Claire's words left Luna feeling blue.

Pine Street was bustling with activity by the time they arrived.

"Check out that truck!" Justin shouted. He ran to inspect the bright red fire truck parked at the end of the street. The firemen were there to make sure that Melody's jumps observed safety regulations.

"Hi, girls!" Melody had raced from her trailer to Luna and Claire. She was wearing thick parachute gear and her silver moon-jumping boots. Her hair had been premessed and her face was presmudged. She looked funny. But she did not seem to mind.

"For the first time, the makeup people made me look worse instead of better," she said. "I wish it could be like that more often."

For a moment, Luna saw a wistful shadow pull over Melody's face. Only for a moment, though.

"Hey, Melody," said Claire. "Can we look at the fire truck?"

"Sure!" Melody's dimpled smile flashed. "Let's go!"

"Where's Dolores?" asked Luna. Usually Dolores was right there waiting for her, so that they could make a quick getaway. Dolores did not like to spend a second longer than she had to on her sister's movie set.

"She's off sulking," Melody said over her shoulder, "because Dad can't take you two to the Rare Flower Show. He wants to watch my jumps instead, to make sure they go smooth."

"Oh." Luna was disappointed. But she bet Dolores was even sadder. She had been looking forward to the Flower Show.

Luna pushed through the crowd, searching for Dolores. She checked the trailer. She checked the wardrobe department. She checked the back lot where the crew hung out.

Dolores was nowhere.

Then Willa called, "Places!" and "Quiet on the set!"

Claire and Justin had found a good place to observe the action, standing on the flatbed of the fire truck. Claire signaled for Luna to join them.

After one more scan for Dolores, Luna hoisted herself reluctantly into the truck.

"Action!" called Willa.

Everyone's eyes were trained on Melody as she jumped off a wooden ledge that had been specially constructed for the stunt. Her parachute popped and bloomed open as she landed with a bounce on the trampoline, then another bounce onto the street for her final close-up.

Each time, it looked perfect. But not perfect enough for Willa.

"Take two!" she called. "Take three! Take four! Take five!"

By the sixth take, Melody seemed weary.

"Look happy after you land, Melody," Willa suggested. "Say something like, 'Hooray!' okay?"

"Okay," said Melody tiredly.

Movies even take the fun out of fun, thought Luna.

Then Luna spied Mr. G sitting in a chair next to Willa. He was leaning forward, craning his neck to watch Melody. "Excellent jumping, Mellie," he called.

"Crumbs, Dolores might be *lost*," Luna muttered to Claire, "and all anyone cares about is Melody's jumps."

"Oh, please. Dolores isn't *lost*," said Claire. "I bet she took a walk to let off some steam."

Luna thought on that. "I think Dolores went farther away than a walk, Clairsie," said Luna. "My witch-sense has been bothering me."

"Loon, don't be a doomsday prophet," said Claire.

Luna scanned up and down the street. Where could Dolores be? It was getting late, and there weren't many places to hide on this movie set.

Then it struck her. She knew exactly where Dolores had gone.

"Aha!" she said. She jumped down from the fire truck. Before Claire and Justin could ask her where she was going, she sped around the corner of Pine Street to its back alley.

After checking to make sure that nobody had followed her, Luna looked right and left, crooked her finger, and cast:

"My ears are sharp and heart is strong.
To find what's lost, I'll travel long,

And if need be, along for miles!
This spell is stored in one-star files."

Luna closed her eyes and waited for the spell to kick in.

Then, with a leap of energy, Luna-the-dog bounded around the corner.

Unfortunately, she bounded right into the middle of the movie. Melody, her parachute billowing, had just bounced from the trampo-line onto the street.

She looked surprised, then genuinely happy. "Hooray!" she called. "Hey, doggie!"

"Woof! Woof!" barked Luna. Her hair flopped jaggedly over her eyes.

"Cut! Perfect, Melody!" Willa shouted. "But where'd that mutt come from?"

Mutt? Luna barked indignantly.

"*Heere*, doggie!" Luna heard her brother yelp. Uh-oh. Ever since she and Claire got their kittens, Justin had been bugging their parents for a dog. Already he was climbing out of the truck in quick pursuit.

Justin was a fast runner, but Luna-the-dog was faster. She tore down the street in seconds. She felt strong and powerful.

She did not pause to think about how to get to the park. Her sharp dog-sense knew to follow the river, then shortcut up through the woods. The route was mirror-clear in her mind's eye (and a whole lot quicker than the bus).

Hmm. I really must be part Saint Bernard or collie, Luna thought. My sense of dog-direction is terrific!

But her common sense was less terrific. As soon as she saw the sign for Valley Forge Park, Luna bounded excitedly across the highway—and straight into traffic.

Cars honked. People yelled at her. "Dumb dog! Watch where you're going!"

Embarrassed, Luna leaped over the guard rail and did not look back.

Safe inside the park, she ran and ran and ran and ran. Her lungs seemed to be made of iron. It was amazing—she was Superdog! She'd never get tired!

When she came to the lake, Luna paused for a delicious drink of water. Grandy would have been annoyed to hear her make such disgusting slurping noises. But dog rules were different from people rules.

Refreshed, she made a beeline for Mount Misery.

Well, almost a beeline. On the way, Luna spied a monarch butterfly that she felt a happy impulse to chase for a while. She jumped and snapped.

I must be a very young dog to be this goofy! thought Luna. Maybe only six or seven in people years.

As the butterfly fluttered high out of reach, Luna remembered her mission. She turned and ran headlong to Mount Misery, and to the secret cave. But at the entrance, she stopped. The cave had looked dark and uninviting to Luna-the-girl, and Luna-the-dog didn't like it any better.

She barked once, quizzically.

The sound echoed roughly along the

cave's walls. Other than that, silence.

She barked again, louder. Maybe Dolores had not taken the bus and trekked to the park, after all. Or maybe she had gone too deep into the cave to hear Luna's barking? Luna did not want to go into the cave. It looked scary and cold. She snuffled at some foxtail and Queen Anne's lace that sprang tangled along the cave's entrance. She could not pick up any scent of Dolores.

Her sense of smell was still no good.

But Dolores had to be in that cave! Witch-hunches were almost never wrong!

Ears alert, Luna plunged ahead. Her paws padded along the black earth. She heard the faint click of her nails and the pant of her breath. It made her feel unlike herself. It made her feel brave.

The cave forked in two tunneling directions. "Woof!" Luna barked.

"Who's there?" From far away, a voice wobbled.

"Woof!" Luna answered. She followed

her ears and picked up the pace. When the cave narrowed and turned twisty. Luna kept her nose down, sniffing for a trail.

Frustrated, she barked again.

"Hello?" It was Dolores, for sure. "Don't hurt me, whatever you are!"

Quickly, Luna followed the echoes of Dolores's voice to where she finally found her, sitting in a small ball with her arms wrapped around her knees.

When Dolores saw Luna-the-dog, a smile broke across her face and she jumped to her feet.

"Hey, doggie! Where did you come from?" Dolores used her knuckles to rub Luna's head. "You're not wearing a collar. Are you a stray? Gosh, am I glad to see you, ole boy."

Ole *boy*? Luna whined. She did not like being mistaken for a boy dog.

"I was getting kinda scared," Dolores confessed. "But now you're here to rescue me! And I always wanted a dog. Of course, we can't have one because of my allergies. But if I had one, I'd name him Timbuktu. How 'bout it, ole boy?" Dolores chucked Luna under the chin. "You like the name Timbuktu?"

Timbuktu? Luna whined again. No, she didn't like that name at all.

"Okay, lead me out of here, Timbuktu!" said Dolores.

But Luna did not know how to lead either of them anywhere. She could not pick up the trail. She walked in a slow circle, then flopped down next to Dolores to think.

"Hey, what are you doing?" Dolores put her hands on her hips. "What kind of dog are you? Don't you know how to get us out?"

Luna lifted her head and looked away, mortified. Obviously, if she had a *real* dog nose, she would have followed it back out of the cave, no problem. But to lead by her *Luna* nose . . . impossible. She sighed and scratched behind her ear.

"Come on, ole boy! Take me home!" Now it was Dolores who was whining.

Luna didn't budge. After a minute,

Dolores settled into a despondent lump on the cave's floor. "Gosh. You don't know the way out of here, either, Timbuktu," she said, sounding frightened. "Oh, well, it's not your fault. You're just a dumb dog. Guess we'll wait for my dad or the police. Or something."

Luna put a paw of sympathy on Dolores's knee. In response, Dolores sneezed. Its echo sounded like a thousand sneezes.

"My rock collection is fantastic, even if I didn't find a fossil today," Dolores said in the same nervous voice. "Not to brag, but I just know one day I'll become a world-renowned geologist! And then people won't see me as the sister of talented Melody Malady."

Luna wished she could talk, so that she could tell Dolores her secret: that she didn't think Melody was so talented.

Then again, a talking dog probably would have scared Dolores.

Dolores sneezed again.

Some help I am, Luna thought. I can't make a real rescue, and Dolores is allergic to me.

They sat together in silence. Every second, the cave seemed to grow colder and darker. They sat for so long that Luna began to daydream about chasing squirrels.

"I wonder if anyone's even noticed that I'm lost," said Dolores.

I noticed, thought Luna indignantly. *Not that I'll get any credit.*

Suddenly, Luna's ear pricked up. What was that noise?

There it was again, from far outside. "I swear, Mr. G, I'm not making it up!" shrilled the voice. "She told me it was somewhere over here by Miserable Mountain, or whatever it's called."

Claire!

Luna sat up. She barked and barked and barked and barked. She knew what had happened. Claire had remembered about the secret cave, and had led everyone to it.

"Hey, I think I hear Lu—I mean, I think I hear a dog!" shouted Claire. Her witch-sense had recognized Luna's bark.

"I don't hear anything," Mr. G's voice was worried.

Luna nudged Dolores to get up.

"Whadda ya hear, Timbugtu?" asked Dolores. Her voice sounded stuffy. As she jumped to her feet, she doubled over in another sneeze. "You wad be to follow you?"

Luna barked some more. She nosed Dolores to move along. Yes, she had to be part Border collie.

"Ogay, Timbugtu. Lead be oud!" said Dolores happily.

Luna barked for Claire to keep talking.

"We're out here!" called Claire. "Yoo-hoo! The park ranger says look up."

Luna looked up. For the first time, she saw the glow-in-the-dark arrows pointing the way out. So they had never been in danger, after all. The signs were there all along!

Confidently, she trotted ahead, barking, with Dolores close on her heels. They stumbled out into the late afternoon sun.

A big crowd was there to meet them.

Claire, Justin, Melody, Mr. G, a green-suited park ranger, and even Willa had all come to look for Dolores.

"Dolores!" squeaked Melody. "We were so worried!" And she ran over to give her twin a hug.

Dolores looked embarrassed, but she seemed pleased to be the center of attention for once.

"Guess we're gonna have to paint another set of glow dots even lower," said the park ranger, "for our smaller visitors."

Mr. G lifted Dolores into the air, squeezed her hard, and set her down. "Dolores, kiddo, you had a lot of people scared."

"Bud I wuddn't sgared!—*achoo!* Timbugtu was—*achoo*—wib me!" wheezed Dolores. "Where's Luna?"

"She, um, said she was going to go look for you at the flower show. She told me to look for you here," Claire answered.

Dolores nodded. "I shuddn't hab gone widdout delling sombuddy."

"Lucky that Timbugtu was around!" Claire winked at her twin. "Loyal and trustworthy to the end."

"I wonder whose dog he is?" Justin crouched down and looked into Luna's eyes. "I feel like I've seen it around the neighborhood."

"He looks like a lot of dogs," said Claire quickly.

Justin wrinkled his nose. "Mangy old thing. He needs to spend a few hours at the pet groomer," he said. "Someone gave him a real bad homemade haircut."

"Hey, I like his haircut," said Claire. She threw an arm down around Luna as they walked to the car. "Nice work, sis," she whispered.

As if in imitation, Melody put her arm around Dolores. "I was worried about you, Dolores," she said. "Jess and Bess help each other out so much in *Double Delight*, I think maybe I should take some pointers from them."

"Nod to brag," said Dolores with a sneeze, "but I'b preddy iddepeddend."

To Luna's dog ears, though, Dolores did not sound that independent. She still sounded scared. And Luna thought she detected something soft in Melody's eyes as she looked at her sister.

It was only for a moment, but it was too real to be an act.

9
Wrap and Print

OCTOBER HAD ARRIVED. The real October, not a movie-set version. It was a red-gold leaves and apple crisp October, and Claire loved-loved-loved it.

"Just think! We've been sixth graders for six weeks! Think about it! Sixth graders!" Claire leaned back and stretched contentedly.

She and Luna were sitting in the cafeteria eating butterscotch brownies with their friends

Alexa, Adam, and Courtney. It was a cafeteria tradition at Tower Hill Middle School to celebrate the sixth week of sixth grade with butterscotch brownies. (The cafeteria staff also celebrated five weeks of fifth grade with peanut-butter brownies, and seventh-week seventh graders got rocky-road brownies.)

"We are no longer middle school novices!" said Claire. *Novice* was one of her favorite new words. It was a fancier way of saying "beginner."

Claire had been using it a lot today.

"Not to brag, but I've felt like a sixth grader for a long time," said Luna. "Ever since the last day of fifth grade, in fact. And it's not like we changed much. We're still at Tower Hill Middle. We go to the same gym and auditorium. The only thing different is now you and Alexa have Mr. Lee for a teacher and Courtney, Adam, and I have Mrs. Shaw."

Claire thought her sister was being a bit persnickety as usual, but she was too happy to care. After all, not only was today their "six weeks of sixth grade" anniversary, but tonight was the opening of Melody Malady's movie.

In honor of the occasion, Claire had worn her gold shirt and her gold hat with the feather to school.

"Claire, are you *sure* that's the same gold outfit that Melody wore on her show?" Alexa asked.

"Of course," Claire answered. She dropped her last bite of butterscotch brownie into her mouth and swallowed it down with some apple cider from the jug that she had brought with her lunch.

"It could be a copy," said Courtney. "They sell those knockoffs everywhere at the mall."

"Oh, who needs you, doubtful doubters," scoffed Claire. "All I can say is, it's not a knock-off copy of *me* in the movie. 'Mom, can I have some hot apple cider?'" She recited her line from the movie once again for the pure pleasure of it.

"Ugh," groaned Alexa, reaching for another

brownie. "If I have to hear you say that one more time . . ."

"But I need people to recognize me. I don't want to be a novice movie star," said Claire with another swig.

"We *all* recognize you, Claire," said Adam. "You've shown us the picture from *Philadelphia Now!* a thousand times. Next thing you'll be saying is that you and Melody are pen pals."

Claire shrugged and patted her pocket, where she was carrying a letter from Melody Malady.

In the letter, Melody had written that *The Melody Malady Show* had been canceled and that she probably wouldn't be doing any more movies for a while. She said her mom and dad wanted her to concentrate on being a real kid. She didn't seem too upset about it. But she had specially asked Claire not to read her letter to any of her friends, since it was a private, noncelebrity letter.

Claire didn't mind. Being a witch, she

was used to keeping big secrets. She would never in a billion years show Melody's letter around.

Anyway, her friends might say that she faked the letter, too!

That evening, the twins, Justin, their mother and Steve, their father and Fluffy, and even Grandy and Grampy all went to the Ritz Theater to see Melody's movie.

"Although I have no idea why I would waste my time with a G-rated movie," groused Grandy as they waited in the ticket line. "That means no fun parts."

"Mother!" Jill Bundkin frowned.

"Pay attention to the leaves," said Justin. "That's all my work."

"Even if this movie is a blockbuster," said Claire, "Melody Malady won't be in the public eye for a while. So I guess that means this is my last movie, too."

"I'm glad," said their father. "You only had to meet Melody once to know she was under too much pressure."

"I'm glad, too," said Luna. "It was awful enough when Claire was a *pretend* movie star. Imagine if she turned into a real one?"

Justin made gagging sounds. Claire tossed her head. Doubtful doubters.

The whole family filed into the theater and into one long row.

The lights went dark as the previews started. Claire sank back into her seat with a thrill. She hoped that the camera loved her. Having the camera love you was an important part of being a celebrity.

The music for the feature presentation began. Melody Malady's name scrolled across the screen in sweeping letters. Claire felt a burst of pride for her newfound friend. Melody Malady was awesome!

Double Delight opened with a rainstorm, followed by Jess and Bess's orphanage scenes. Those parts had been filmed in Hollywood and were fun to watch, since Claire had never seen them before.

Then came the part when Jess and Bess were adopted by villains, and they moved to Philadelphia. The camera panned over the sky-line.

"Hello, Philly!" yelled Justin. A few other people in the audience clapped and whooped.

Claire tensed. The café scene was next, and here it was! The camera zoomed in for a long close-up of Melody drinking from a mug of hot apple cider. She was smiling her perfect-perfect-perfect dimpled smile. "Mmm. This is good cider," she said.

Then the scene was over.

Claire leaned forward. "Hey!" she whispered loudly. "Did I miss myself? Was I in that? Did you hear anyone say 'Mom, I want some hot apple cider'?"

"Shhh! They must have cut it out!" hissed Justin. He made scissors of his fingers. "Snip, snip!"

No! Claire could not believe it.

The scene probably was in another part of the movie. Claire strained every eye muscle, hardly daring to blink, salamander-style, in case she missed herself.

She salamander-watched the scene where Bess saved Jess from the robber.

She salamander-watched the scene where Jess saved Bess from the kidnapper.

Now they were coming up to the moon boots and parachute scene.

Claire was beginning to be alarmed. The moon boots scene meant the end of the movie. Claire watched the screen as Melody seemed to jump effortlessly through the sky. As she landed with a swish and bounce, a dog tore into view.

"Hooray!" called Melody. A huge, dimpled smile appeared on her face as she bent and hugged the dog.

"Woof! Woof!" barked the dog in a long, Luna-eyed close-up.

Claire's eyes narrowed.

They'd cut out Claire's café scene, but added a Luna-the-dog scene?

No way!

But it was true.

Now the movie was finished. The credits rolled. Claire La Dare's name flashed up in a long list of other names. Justin Bundkin's name appeared with the crew.

Needles and newts' eyes! She had been completely cut from the movie.

"I was nowhere!" Claire moaned as they left the theater. Bitterly she crunched the real October leaves in her path. "And I didn't even use my real name! So nobody will believe anything!"

"But they'll see my real name, ha ha!" Justin yelled as he raced by. "Hey, Mom, can we have some hot apple cider? Right now I'm really in the mood for some hot apple cider!"

"Be quiet, Justin!" Claire protested. "Why do you have to tease me every second?"

"'Cause I can!" yelled Justin. "I'm the oldest!"

"That dog looked suspiciously familiar," Grandy remarked. She had crept up on the

117

twins. She shook her silver-handled pigeon-shooing cane that she always brought to the city.

"What do you mean, Grandy?" asked Luna innocently, but there was no fooling a five-star witch.

"What I mean, Luna, is that you almost forfeit your half-star and spy globes when you appeared in that movie," said Grandy. "The Decree Keepers told me to warn you: stay out of the spotlight." In her palm, however, appeared the two small, crystal spheres. They were baseball-sized and not at all magical-looking. But Claire and Luna knew better.

"Our spy globes!" they cried together.

"Good work with your Samaritan Spells," Grandy acknowledged, as she handed one to each twin. "You are officially one-and-a-half-star witches. But don't let me catch you doing pet tricks on the big screen again!"

With that, she stalked ahead to take Grampy's arm.

Luna shook her globe. "Show me

Dolores," she said. The twins watched as the globe swirled with colors that faded to produce an image of Dolores in the globe. She was sitting at a desk, looking through a stamp album.

"Hmm. I guess she's moved on to other hobbies," said Luna.

"Cool," said Claire, shaking her globe. "With these globes, we can spy on anyone." She peered into it. "Show me my best friend!"

"Where?" Luna peered into Claire's globe.

Her own face stared back at her.

"It's me," she said.

"Of course it's you," said Claire. "Why do you sound surprised?"

"I was looking for Melody," admitted Luna. "I thought she was your best friend. Since she's a movie star, and all."

Claire was shocked. She stopped still on the pavement and looked into her identical twin sister's identically brown eyes. "Crumbs, Luna. Are you kidding? I wouldn't trade you for all the celebrities in Hollywood! We're not just twins! We're best friends for life!" she exclaimed.

Luna smiled. "Best friends for life!" she agreed.

And they hooked pinkies on it.

MH

NO 30 '03

BC

FE 15 '04

FO

NY 15 '04

DL

NO 15 '04

BG

MY 15 '04

J Gri

Griffin, Adele.

Witch twins and melody
malady /
MH 33500007675416